Acting Edition

Young Americans

by Lauren Yee

SAMUEL FRENCH

No one shall make any changes in this title(s) for the purpose of production. No part of this book may be reproduced, stored in a retrieval system, scanned, uploaded, or transmitted in any form, by any means, now known or yet to be invented, including mechanical, electronic, digital, photocopying, recording, videotaping, or otherwise, without the prior written permission of the publisher. No one shall share this title(s), or any part of this title(s), through any social media or file hosting websites.

For all inquiries regarding motion picture, television, online/digital and other media rights, please contact Concord Theatricals Corp.

MUSIC AND THIRD-PARTY MATERIALS USE NOTE

Licensees are solely responsible for obtaining formal written permission from copyright owners to use copyrighted music and/or other copyrighted third-party materials (e.g. artworks, logos) in the performance of this play and are strongly cautioned to do so. If no such permission is obtained by the licensee, then the licensee must use only original music and materials that the licensee owns and controls. Licensees are solely responsible and liable for clearances of all third-party copyrighted materials, including without limitation music, and shall indemnify the copyright owners of the play(s) and their licensing agent, Concord Theatricals Corp., against any costs, expenses, losses and liabilities arising from the use of such copyrighted third-party materials by licensees. For music, please contact the appropriate music licensing authority in your territory for the rights to any incidental music.

IMPORTANT BILLING AND CREDIT REQUIREMENTS

If you have obtained performance rights to this title, please refer to your licensing agreement for important billing and credit requirements.

YOUNG AMERICANS was originally co-produced by Portland Center Stage (Marissa Wolf, Artistic Director; Liam Kaas-Lentz, Managing Director) and Pittsburgh Public Theater (Marya Sea Kaminski, Artistic Director; Shaunda McDill, Managing Director).

The Portland Center Stage production of *YOUNG AMERICANS* premiered on February 11, 2023, in the Ellyn Bye Studio in Portland, OR. The production was directed by Desdemona Chiang, with scenic design by Junghyun Georgia Lee, costume design by Susan Tsu, lighting design by Solomon Weisbard, and sound design by Andre Pluess. The production stage manager was Janine Vanderhoff. The cast was as follows:

JOE...Danny Bernardo
JENNY..Marielle Young
LUCY ....Sammy Rat Rios

The Pittsburgh Public Theater production premiered on April 26, 2023, at the O'Reilly Theater in Pittsburgh, PA. The cast and creative team were the same, with the addition of production stage manager Taylor K. Meszaros.

CHARACTERS

JOE – male, about 30 and about 50, an immigrant
JENNY – female, 20s, his soon-to-be wife, also an immigrant
LUCY – female, 21, an immigrant who came over at a young age

JOE and **JENNY** are played by actors of the same race. **LUCY** is played by an actor of a different race than **JOE** and **JENNY**. None of the characters should be played by white actors.

SETTING

This play is set in the United States.
Two road trips following an identical path.
From Washington, D.C., to Portland, Oregon.

TIME

The present and twenty years earlier.

AUTHOR'S NOTE

The play runs with no intermission.

Prologue

*(**JENNY** speaks to us. here, english is her second language.)*

JENNY. it was something you realized

early on

as a child.

"you will never be happy here."

heavy, am i right?!

quite SOMETHING so young!

"you will never be happy here."

but the flip side?

you were always meant to wander.

this is your curse, to make your roots in sand.

your curse, yeah, but also your strength.

so okay, you think.

why not?

why not see who you have always been meant to be?

Scene 1

*(**LUCY** coming out of the airport gate with her carry-on suitcase. **JOE** intercepts her. she stops in her tracks.)*

JOE. welcome to america!

welcome back.

LUCY. ...

JOE. lucy.

you got nothing to say?

you got nothing to say to your own dad?

what? you go away for a year and you do not remember me?

you forget my face so easily?

LUCY. omigod! dad! DAD. what're you doing here?

did you have a conference, did you –

wait.

JOE. i said i would pick you up from the airport.

LUCY. in portland. you said you would pick me up from the airport in portland. oregon. where you live. this is washington d.c. the other side of the country.

JOE. ah ah ah, i did not say i would pick you up in portland! i said i would pick you up from the airport. i did not say which.

LUCY. why would you do that? i'm flying into portland. i've got a layover and then i'm going to get on a connecting flight TO portland.

JOE. don't worry. your connection, i have cancelled it!

LUCY. what? how?!

JOE. i did not know you could do that. but many things i am learning about airplane travel.

but this way, we save on money.

LUCY. by driving all the way here to get me?

JOE. i read online about carbon footprints! so i drive instead, much better for the planet! recycle reduce reuse, close the lid! you come back, let me drive you home. let me take you home to portland.

LUCY. in which car? your car?

> *(maybe this is a moment to first reveal joe's car?)*

you want to take me all the way across the country in that car?

JOE. same car i always use! same car i drive all the time!

LUCY. is it gonna make it all the way?

JOE. what? junior year abroad and now you too cool to be seen in your dad's old car? you think you gonna seem like a lame-o with me?

LUCY. no –

JOE. what, you think someone see me driving you around, they gonna think i am kidnapping you?

LUCY. well, you kind of are.

JOE. like some pedophile!

LUCY. i'm twenty-one.

JOE. or else i am a good catch! rich man!

LUCY. you couldn't have waited, what, seven more hours, till my plane got into portland?

JOE. why would i wait?

LUCY. so instead you come all the way out here?

JOE. i wanted to be spontaneous! do things i have not done before! hey, you ask me what i wanted to do? this is what i want to do. go on a trip with my daughter! keep me from having a MOFO.

LUCY. a what?

JOE. a MOFO! "the fear of missing out."

LUCY. you mean FOMO.

JOE. no, "MOFO."

LUCY. no, "FOMO." it's an acronym for the "fear of missing out."

JOE. well, i don't want that either! so what do you say?

LUCY. what other choice do i have?

JOE. exactly!

LUCY. *(beat)* fine. it's fine. let's go.

JOE. and that is what i like to hear!

Scene 2

> *(twenty years earlier:* **JOE** *and* **JENNY** *in the car. in their scenes together, they speak in their native language, so no accents. this is the past. their conversation has the vibe of a once promising date gone bad.)*

JOE. *(out of the blue)* that wedding was nice!

JENNY. what?

JOE. that wedding.

JENNY. which wedding?

JOE. the one we just went to.

JENNY. the wedding from six months ago?

JOE. yeah,

JENNY. oh. um. yeah. it was nice.

JOE. that couple seemed like a very nice couple.

JENNY. my cousin just wants to have kids, they'll be fine.

JOE. it's good to see you again!

JENNY. *(beat, then)* you too.

JOE. been a while!

JENNY. six months.

JOE. haven't seen you since that wedding! you didn't run into any trouble, did you?

JENNY. at the airport?

JOE. with customs? paperwork?

JENNY. not really, no.

JOE. so you just like, generally run late.

JENNY. was i late?

JOE. you took a long time to come out.

JENNY. i think i came out in a normal amount of time.

JOE. i almost wasn't sure you'd show!

JENNY. it was a big airport.

JOE. washington dulles! one of the biggest!

JENNY. yeah.

JOE. also! your parents left me a message saying they were going to mail more of your stuff over once we're settled, but i don't think i gave them my mailing address... unless you did?

JENNY. ...no?

JOE. so. that's something we should figure out.

JENNY. yeah.

JOE. are you hungry?

JENNY. we just ate.

JOE. right.

JENNY. are YOU hungry?

JOE. yes.

JENNY. then why didn't you –

JOE. i was trying not to eat so much. first impressions!

JENNY. oh okay –

JOE. can you be quiet for a minute?

JENNY. what?

JOE. i'm trying to concentrate. there's an exit i'm trying to – shoot, i think i missed it.

JENNY. oh. sorry. do you want me to help you –

JOE. no, no, you can just – okay, i think i know where i'm going now.

(silence)

WOW!

JENNY. what?

JOE. WOW! out the window. WOW.

JENNY. what what?!

JOE. you missed it. *(with awe)* it was a bird.

JENNY. oh.

JOE. i'm a bird watcher. oregon's a good place for that. here's not so bad either, if you're interested in learning.

JENNY. okay.

JOE. once i moved to oregon, i got really into it.

JENNY. i can tell.

JOE. one thing i found amazing – when i first started – is that people think we've already discovered all the birds out there, when that is actually not the case.

JENNY. okay.

JOE. what is ACTUALLY the case is that there are SO MANY more birds out that no one's ever seen before. *(corrects)* or that people have seen before, but no one's NOTED, officially. so they're still technically undiscovered.

JENNY. so how do you "discover" a bird?

JOE. well, you see it. and you write it down. and if it's a bird no one's ever described before, that's yours! you found it!

JENNY. oh.

(a lull. the silence bothers her.)

so i hear you're also into music?

JOE. what? no?

JENNY. oh.

JOE. no, i do. i do like music. i just didn't know what you were asking.

JENNY. oh.

> *(silence)*

JOE. *(realizes)* did you want to play music?

JENNY. we don't have to.

JOE. no! music, music.

> *(he pushes in a tape. top 40 music of the era plays.*)*

JENNY. thanks, j–

JOE. *(stops her)* joe. you can call me joe.

JENNY. what?

JOE. now that we're here. that's my name, here. "joe." i chose it myself!

JENNY. oh.

JOE. i mean, i still have my actual name, you can call me that, if you prefer.

JENNY. no, that's fine, "joe."

JOE. you might want to think about what you want people to call you.

JENNY. i already have a name.

JOE. an american name.

---

*A license to produce *Young Americans* does not include a performance license for any third-party or copyrighted music. Licensees should create an original composition or use music in the public domain. For further information, please see the Music and Third-Party Materials Use Note on page iii.

ideally, something people will have positive associations with.

"joe montana."

"joe dimaggio."

JENNY. "joseph stalin."

JOE. "joe namath."

your name's too hard and they won't even bother to mispronounce it, they'll just stop saying it, is what i've found. they'll just go like, "professor!" or "hey!" or "morning," or just skip you over entirely. that's why: joe. everyone knows joe. it also serves as a kind of act of good faith. like –

"i am here."

"i am you."

"i am just like you."

"joe."

JENNY. i'll think about it.

JOE. "jenny."

JENNY. ...

JOE. what do you think of "jenny?"

JENNY. does it have good connotations? who're the famous jennys?

JOE. well, "jenny lind."

"jenny mccarthy."

"jenny...craig?"

not so many famous jennys. *(admits)* not so many famous women.

(**JOE** *off in his own thoughts –*)

JOE. how many kids do you think?

JENNY. do i think what?

JOE. how many do you think we'll have? *(adds)* not right now. later. together. for the interview. when they ask us.

JENNY. do we have to match?

JOE. not necessarily, no, but –

JENNY. i already got my visa. i passed.

JOE.   the first test. but to stay here? to stay married – i mean, once we get married –

JENNY. we've got ninety days. we don't have to get married for ninety days, right?

JOE. but it'll come up fast. we've got to make sure we know our story, how we met –

JENNY. so how did we meet?

JOE. *(confused)* we met at that wedding six months ago.

JENNY. okay, we met at that wedding six months ago.

JOE. *(joke)* at least i did!

JENNY. *(shrugs)* i'll say whatever you want me to say. how many kids? give me a number, i'll say it.

JOE. you shouldn't look at it like that.

JENNY. what do you need to know?

JOE. do you want girls or boys? or do you not yet have a preference? if you don't yet, that's okay.

JENNY. are they gonna ask us this?

JOE. you never know!

JENNY. do YOU have a preference?

JOE. girls.

JENNY. liar.

JOE. not lying!

JENNY. boys, you don't have to worry about. girls? girls are trouble. nothing but trouble.

JOE. but i love girls. i always wanted a younger sister. better than boys! you may not know now, but you'll develop a preference.

JENNY. or not.

JOE. all girls want kids. it's biologically proven.

even if you don't think you do, you do!

it's what you were made to do.

i mean, not like YOU YOU, but

you have breasts.

you have hips.

you have a, you know.

JENNY. you assume.

JOE. it's the one thing you were made to do.

more than anything else.

more than typing or making cookies or driving in a car.

it would be a subversion of your biology otherwise.

JENNY. mmm.

JOE. i always wanted to take this trip. when i got the job at PSU, i was planning to drive cross country, but schedule and all, i didn't want to be late, so that didn't happen. *(thinks)* and that would've been such a lonely trip, you know?

JENNY. you don't like driving by yourself?

JOE. also i figured this could be like, our honeymoon!

JENNY. our what?

JOE. our – *(thinks)* "trip you take once you're married."

JENNY. we're not married yet.

JOE. yet.

JENNY. so doesn't that come after?

JOE. give us a chance to get to know each other! doing something that's new for both of us. that's important, actually. i read somewhere that shared experiences – where the experience is new for both parties – help to form lasting emotional bonds, SO the best way to speed up any relationship is to go on a trip together because then you are both taken out of your comfort zone and forced to confront a set of new circumstances that triggers your long-term memory in more profound ways. you might say it accelerates the relationship!

> *(she begins to drift off to sleep.)*

what about you? have you ever heard that before?

> *(no response)*

have you? *(louder)* ever heard that?

JENNY. *(startled awake)* what?!

JOE. were you asleep?

JENNY. yeah.

JOE. you wanna sleep? you should sleep.

JENNY. thanks.

> *(she leans her chair back, closes her eyes. he drives, then –)*

JOE. are you cold? *(louder)* are you cold? or not cold enough?

> *(he shifts the air flow of the a/c.)*

JENNY. i'm fine.

JOE. are you sure? i can turn it higher. OR OFF! i can also turn it off.

JENNY. right there, is perfect.

JOE. okay.

(she closes her eyes again.)

goodnight! goodNAP!

(then as she sleeps…)

virginia.

virginia.

virginia.

virginia.

virginia.

virginia.

virginia.

virginia.

TENNESSEE!

(she wakes with a start.)

JENNY. what?!

JOE. state lines. we crossed the state line. WELCOME TO AMERICA!

Scene 3

*(music similar to "sexyback" plays from a cassette tape. **JOE** hums along.*)*

LUCY. omigod.

JOE. i like this justin timberlake so much. he seems to have done very well for someone who seems like a total asshole! he is bringing sexy back. i did not know it was gone, but that is why there is a song, yes?

LUCY. he's a little before my time.

JOE. what?! JT?! noooo!

LUCY. that song is how old?

JOE. NOOOOOO. it was just on the radio the other day, wow.

*(**JOE** continues to hum to himself.)*

look at this! look at us. thelma and louise! reunited at last!

LUCY. i've only been gone for a year.

JOE. but what a year!

LUCY. junior year abroad. people go abroad, it's not that weird.

JOE. you leave me to manage alone!

---

* A license to produce *Young Americans* does not include a performance license for "Sexyback." The publisher and author suggest that the licensee contact ASCAP or BMI to ascertain the music publisher and contact such music publisher to license or acquire permission for performance of the song. If a license or permission is unattainable for "Sexyback," the licensee may not use the song in *Young Americans* but should create an original composition in a similar style or use a similar song in the public domain. For further information, please see the Music and Third-Party Materials Use Note on page iii.

LUCY. you weren't alone. what about that kid you hired? kevin?

JOE. kevin has been a disaster.

LUCY. kevin's fifteen.

JOE. he is sixteen now. and still very lacking.

i have him watching the shop this week.

i am very concerned.

LUCY. then you should've stayed home.

JOE. and the birds do not like him.

LUCY. you don't know that.

JOE. oh no, you can tell! as soon as he walks in? they shit all over him.

LUCY. i thought that was supposed to be lucky. you told me that was lucky.

JOE. he won't work late, won't work weekends!

LUCY. he's in high school.

JOE. YOU would work late and work weekends when you were in high school!

LUCY. i know.

JOE. i do not know how we found him, he is incompetent.

LUCY. that's why you should hire a REAL employee.

JOE. but move over, kevin! *(re:* **LUCY***)* there is a new old sheriff back in town!

LUCY. mm yeah.

JOE. *(stops)* which way do we go?

LUCY. hold on.

(**LUCY** *tries to check the directions with her phone. she searches for reception.)*

JOE. see, i told you! a phone it will go in and out, but a map you can trust forever!

LUCY. where's the map?

(**LUCY** *finds an old map in the glove compartment. full of pencil markings and post-it flags.*)

what is this?

JOE. this is our route!

(**LUCY** *examines the old map.*)

LUCY. oh ho ho.

JOE. what?

LUCY. "i can be spontaneous! i can do things i haven't done before."

JOE. i can!

LUCY. you've done this road trip before.

JOE. when have you and i done this before?

(**LUCY** *holds up the old map.*)

LUCY. you did this trip before you got married.

JOE. what?!

LUCY. is this the exact same route?

JOE. no. yes. maybe. why? what is wrong with that?

LUCY. wasn't it an awful trip?

JOE. what?! who said that?

LUCY. you've got us going through arkansas. idaho.

JOE. what is wrong with idaho? idaho is a great place! so many potatoes! so many western bars! you like to dance? in idaho, you will dance.

LUCY. if you say so.

JOE. it was a great trip. you will see. i will show you all the notable places we went to.

LUCY. such as –?

JOE. many places you would not know of.

LUCY. you didn't even go to the grand canyon.

JOE. grand canyon! who wants to go to the grand canyon? everyone goes to the grand canyon. "wow, a big hole." whereas my road trip? one of a kind, unique!

LUCY. yeah, full of nothing states and tourist traps.

JOE. four corners is a tourist trap?

LUCY. well, it's a man-made tourist site.

JOE. four things at once! you will see. you stand there, you are in four places at once! what could be more exciting?

*(**LUCY** points to one marked flag on the map.)*

LUCY. what's this?

JOE. IHOPE.

LUCY. where?

JOE. IHOPE. with the whipped cream, the waffles?!

LUCY. you want to go to the international house of pancakes?

JOE. YES!

LUCY. you know they have those at home.

JOE. but not THE IHOPE. long time ago, i go to this IHOPE, i get kicked out for life! never to return, but ha HA, twenty years later, i am back, bitches.

LUCY. it's called IHOP.

JOE. i know.

LUCY. then why would you –

JOE. "IHOPE." i like it better. it is a much more american thing to say. first time we pass by IHOPE –

LUCY. – IHOP –

JOE. i see the sign, i say to myself, "wow, that is the best name for a restaurant, we need to go there STAT." and then i learn it is called IHOP. and i think, "wow, what a terrible name for a restaurant, that makes no sense." "i hop for what?" so no, i will not call it by this name. i will call it by the name it should have: "I HOPE." *(beat)* maybe they even have "kids eat free" still. we can ask.

LUCY. i'm not asking them if i can eat for free.

JOE. you are my kid. you eat free.

LUCY. they're not going to give it to you.

JOE. what? they need to see proof i am your dad?

LUCY. no. i mean, i'm a junior in college. i don't think i qualify anymore.

JOE. you are my kid. you will eat free.

Scene 4

(**JOE** *and* **JENNY** *in the car*)

JOE. so nashville: the state capital, it was founded in 1779 by a party of overmountain men, which is a kind of frontiersman. their state flower is the purple passionflower and the iris, so very purple. their state bird is the mockingbird. their state fruit is the tomato –

(the tape in the tape deck ends. silence.)

oh, can you flip the tape over?

JENNY. you want to listen to it again?

JOE. yeah.

*(***JENNY*** flips the cassette tape over.)*

repetition is a great way to learn a new language, ESPECIALLY if it's music because music, apparently, embeds itself into your brain in a SLIGHTLY different place than regular language, which should help with learning english.

JENNY. i'm pretty good with linguistics. i speak three languages.

JOE. yeah, but english? english's hard. you'll see. it's all borrowed from everywhere else, so a lot of it DOES NOT MAKE SENSE.

JENNY. okay, then i just won't learn english.

JOE. noooo, you have to.

JENNY. why?

JOE. because! what're you gonna do instead? just wave your hands up and down or something?

JENNY. if that works. i don't have to learn english to live here.

JOE. ummm. yeahhh. yeah, you do. you do. if you want to succeed here, you kind of do.

and there are so many variations and which variation you choose says EVERYTHING about your meaning, your intentions. like if you wanted to say, "i am in portland," there are so many ways you could say it.

JENNY. how many ways are there?

JOE. like –

"i have been in portland."

"i have been to portland."

"i go to portland."

"i live in portland."

"i am living in portland."

"i am from portland."

JENNY. or just "i am in portland?"

JOE. SO MANY WAYS.

JENNY. "i am in portland" seems to cover it.

JOE. but you say that: do you live here? is this your home? are you here for a day, a week, a year? forever? these imply very different relationships to the city of portland!

JENNY. so when are we getting to portland? are we close yet?

JOE. to portland?

JENNY. yeah.

JOE. ha HA, nah.

JENNY. but hasn't it been –

JOE. portland's on the other side of the country.

JENNY. ?!?

JOE. where did you think it was?

JENNY. near new york?

JOE. portland?!

JENNY. on the map –

JOE. OH! you mean portland, MAINE. see, portland, OREGON –

JENNY. – there are two portlands? –

JOE. yes. portland, OREGON, that's where we're going. that's where i work. *(thinks to himself, "ha HA")* portland, MAINE!

JENNY. are they different?

JOE. if i took you to portland, MAINE, wouldn't be much of a road trip!

JENNY. a what?

JOE. a road trip!

JENNY. what is – "a road trip"?

JOE. it's a trip! that's not necessarily going TO anywhere.

JENNY. i thought we were GOING TO portland.

JOE. we are. but a trip where the destination isn't the point, it's more like, the ROAD you're going on IS the trip. *(gestures around him)* like this is it.

JENNY. this is the exciting part?

JOE. yes! and portland, OREGON is an incredible place, you'll see.

JENNY. you really like portland, don't you?

JOE. it's good for what i do.

JENNY. you teach...city planning?

JOE. urban studies. not city planning.

JENNY. must be nice, being your own boss.

JOE. not really.

JENNY. you walk into that classroom, no one tells you what to do.

JOE. uh, many people all the time tell me exactly what to do. if not the dean, then the chair. if not the chair, then the students. it's not great.

JENNY. if it's not great, just leave. get a new job.

JOE. it's not that easy.

JENNY. yeah, it's not easy, but it's not impossible.

JOE. getting this job was pretty much impossible. there aren't a plethora of universities clamoring for me.

JENNY. but you chose portland.

JOE. i chose portland because portland chose me.

JENNY. you can sign up for classes at the school, right?

JOE. at PSU?

JENNY. audit?

JOE. in what?

JENNY. in something. i haven't decided yet.

JOE. well, i think you would need to be more specific than just wanting to take classes in "something." for "whatever."

JENNY. as i'm figuring out what to do.

JOE. "what to do?"

JENNY. for work.

JOE. work?

JENNY. what else am i gonna do?

JOE. well, you know – you might get busy –

JENNY. with what?

JOE. *(beat)* you know.

Scene 5

    (**JOE** *drives.*)

JOE. i spy with my little eye, a tree.

LUCY. you just told me what it is.

JOE. but WHICH tree?

LUCY. that one.

JOE. damn, you are good.

    (in the lull, the music in the car becomes more
    present. something with a long instrumental*
    vamp. they hum along. it gets elaborate. then –)

bird bird!

LUCY. where where?

JOE. three-thirty-five!

    (**LUCY** *clocks the bird. tracks it as it flies away.*)

LUCY. got it.

JOE. redheaded woodpecker?

LUCY. yellow-bellied sapsucker.

JOE. NO.

LUCY. gotta check the belly.

JOE. i will be damned.

    (a quiet reverence between them)

LUCY. you know it's weird.

---

*A license to produce *Young Americans* does not include a performance
license for any third-party or copyrighted music. Licensees should create
an original composition or use music in the public domain. For further
information, please see the Music and Third-Party Materials Use Note
on page iii.

JOE. what?! what is weird?

LUCY. i figured i'd see you and you'd have, like, a million questions.

JOE. about what?

LUCY. you haven't seen me in a year.

JOE. ten months, six days, and – *(checks time)* three hours!

LUCY. you know you can ask.

JOE. what is there to ask?

LUCY. you ask about everything else.

JOE. me?! when have i –?!

LUCY. "what're you doing?"

"where are you going?"

"how was your date?"

"was that a date?"

"how was your friend?"

"who is your friend?"

"who is your friend's friend driving the car?"

"how you know they can drive?"

"you see their license?"

"you take a picture?"

JOE. yeah! good question! you don't got a license? you should not drive!

LUCY. so nothing here, huh?

JOE. okay. fine. how was it?

LUCY. good.

JOE. bet they did not have coffee!

LUCY. they had coffee. i didn't go for a whole year without coffee.

JOE. or the food! portland, you cannot beat the food!

LUCY. they also had food.

JOE. but did they have food that you had to stand in a parking lot for?

LUCY. okay. no. they didn't have that.

JOE. other places, they put food in restaurants. only in portland will you get your food in a parking lot!

LUCY. i know you missed me –

JOE. psh! miss you? you want to spend your junior year abroad seeing where you are from, where you were born? okay! why not! see where you are from, it is the most natural thing to do.

    (beat)

LUCY. why haven't you gone back?

JOE. gone where?

LUCY. to your country.

JOE. this is my country. i am in my country right now.

LUCY. no. like – YOUR country. where you're from.

JOE. "where i am from."

LUCY. where you are from from.

JOE. "where i am from from from…?"

LUCY. the country you were born in!

JOE. OHHHHH.

LUCY. why haven't you ever gone back? you came out here for college and you never went back.

JOE. pshh! of course i have gone back!

LUCY. when?

JOE. once! i went back once. before we got you.

LUCY. to find a bride? that doesn't count.

JOE. "to find a bride?" what is this, the middle ages of europe? i went and i met your mom.

LUCY. you went back TO meet her.

JOE. that is the same thing.

LUCY. no, it's not.

JOE. i went back once and i did what i needed to do. so why else would i go back? aah, too many cars, too much traffic, everyone in your business! i do not miss any of it, believe you me. here is where i am supposed to be. where i am from one country and you are from another – and yet! here we are. both of us. together. seeing our country. now let us go find a roadside restaurant!

Scene 6

(coming out of a drivethru. **JENNY** *peers inside the restaurant.)*

JENNY. see! look! there're tables. BOOTHS.

JOE. this is faster.

JENNY. i'm gonna spill.

JOE. please don't spill. i just cleaned the mats.

JENNY. well, can we go inside then?

JOE. you wanted to experience a drivethru. this is a drivethru!

JENNY. and now i want to go inside and eat my dinner on a table, not my lap.

JOE. next time we'll go in. next time. we should get a move on anyway, get into nashville before it gets dark.

*(***JOE*** *starts driving away. they eat.)*

JENNY. this has pickles in it.

JOE. does it?

JENNY. you didn't tell them not to?

JOE. you can just take them out.

JENNY. did you not tell them no pickles?

JOE. they never understand my english over the speaker!

JENNY. i thought this was america. you ask for something, they have to give it to you, right?

JOE. here, i'll take it out.

JENNY. *(drops her burger)* fuck.

JOE. here, have mine.

JENNY. what're you gonna eat?

JOE. i'll just eat the fries. i wasn't really hungry anyway. AND i'm driving.

JENNY. omigod, it's a calvin klein.

JOE. *(confused)* what?!

JENNY. it's a CALVIN KLEIN. pull over.

JOE. please don't distract me.

JENNY. we have to go.

JOE. *(looks up quickly)* it's just an outlet store.

JENNY. a what?

JOE. where they put all the old calvin klein clothes, on discount. so it's cheaper.

JENNY. CHEAPER CALVIN KLEIN?!

JOE. it's probably already closed.

JENNY. i don't get to choose anything.

JOE. no. not true.

JENNY. i just want to look. let me look.

JOE. what are you going to do? buy it?

JENNY. yes. maybe, i don't know.

JOE. with what money?

JENNY. you're a professor.

JOE. i'm an adjunct.

JENNY. that's not the same?

JOE. we should really try to save money.

JENNY. so how much money do you not have?

JOE. we should just keep going.

JENNY. *(realizes)* we never get out of this car.

JOE. what? GAS. how do we get gas for the car – and that picture! we took that picture.

JENNY. you mean that picture by that dumb rock.

JOE. that's not getting out of the car?

JENNY. are you afraid? or just poor?

JOE. it's simpler.

JENNY. next thing i want, i'm choosing it.

JOE. so what do you want?

JENNY. i don't know yet. but when i see it, i'm choosing it.

JOE. it doesn't work like that.

JENNY. it does for me.

JOE. well, you have to tell me what it is so i can review it and see if it'll fit into the plan.

JENNY. your plan.

JOE. our, mutual plan. together.

JENNY. that you happen to be in charge of.

JOE. mutually. look, i'm on a very tight timeline. with how long your paperwork took –

JENNY. MY paperwork.

JOE. – how it lined up with my summer break, i can't just drive for however long i want. i have to get us back in time for first day of classes. i can't be late. i mean, my chair is just LOOKING for a reason to get rid of me –

JENNY. the next thing i want, i'm choosing it.

(**JOE** *tries to hide his dismay.*)

JOE. we can talk about it.

JENNY. you know you can't plan for everything!

JOE. i mean, you CAN. i do. HONESTLY – and i just read this somewhere, they've studied this – but honestly, KNOWING what you're going to do and looking forward to it is, scientifically, the best way to experience life. to have the most fun.

JENNY. really.

JOE. like they've done studies and THINKING about a vacation is as much – sometimes even MORE – fun than experiencing it in real time.

JENNY. like this trip?

JOE. yes! like thinking about this trip was actually more fun than this trip really is.

JENNY. tell me about it.

JOE. so if you just choose something, out of the blue, you're never going to have the chance to think about it!

JENNY. well, i choose. i choose what i do not know i want yet.

JOE. that's not going to make you very happy.

JENNY. okay.

JOE. well, let's just get there. we have to get in before dark.

JENNY. says who?

JOE. i don't like driving in the dark.

JENNY. if you're tired, i can drive.

JOE. it's not about being tired!

JENNY. i'm actually a good driver.

JOE. people who're good drivers don't usually say things like, "i'm actually a good driver."

JENNY. i have a license. back home.

JOE. it's a very finicky car.

JENNY. your car is finicky, too. what a surprise.

JOE. what does that mean?

JENNY. it means go right ahead. go drive.

JOE. one day, i'll teach you. one day, you might learn. but tonight, we just focus on getting there. get there, get settled. first night after all!

> *(he drives. silence.)*

JENNY. so: when we get in, how do you want to do it?

JOE. what?

JENNY. *(with meaning.)* when we get in, how do you want to do it? first night.

> *(the car swerves slightly.)*

i just want to know how things are going to go. what you're expecting. so no one's surprised.

JOE. um, i don't – i really hadn't – i mean, we get there, it'll probably be late, you'll probably be tired.

JENNY. i've been sleeping all day.

JOE. we don't have to plan this now!

JENNY. wouldn't it be better to plan now? so we can think about it in advance? if you don't want to –

JOE. NO, i do not want to – i'm driving, i can't really think when i'm driving so – whatever! whatever you want to do, we'll do. it.

JENNY. okay.

JOE. *(beat)* though actually i think we should wait!

JENNY. for what?

JOE. till we get to portland. here, the beds are not nice at the places we're going to stay.

JENNY. why are the beds not nice?

JOE. sometimes they're small or there are insects –

JENNY. why are you taking me to a place that has insects?

JOE. and if we do it out here, then how will we remember that it happened?

JENNY. because it will have happened?

JOE. yeahhhh, but happened where? somewhere that we'll never be again. because they say if you locate memories in places and objects, every time you see it thereafter, you'll think of what it felt like to do it the first time.

JENNY. so: this your first time?

JOE. getting engaged? yes.

JENNY. no, like –

JOE. NO. what?

JENNY. you can say if you haven't.

JOE. of course. of course i've – *(gestures)*

JENNY. okay!

JOE. okay!

JENNY. well, that's solved.

JOE. i have definitely had sexual intercourse before.

JENNY. okay!

Scene 7

(a lull. then –)

JOE. so! you are a lesbian.

LUCY. what?!

JOE. oh. right. *(starts again)* so! you are a lesbian? *(beat)* no homo!

LUCY. don't ever say that again.

JOE. do not worry, real talk, you can be straight with me.

LUCY. real talk? you don't actually want that.

JOE. oh yes i do! i am very interested in what it is like, how *(gestures)* it all works. hey, i gotta ask someone! i try to look it up, i try to ask my questions on the internet, but it was very confusing! and i was on my computer at work, so i do not want to search more in case they think i am looking for porn when i am only looking to learn more about my daughter. so i stopped and thought, "okay, i will ask her instead!"

LUCY. i tell you, what would you do with this?

JOE. hey, maybe i run into a friend on the street, and they say, "hey, how is your daughter, is she a homosexual?" what am i supposed to say? "i don't know"? i cannot say that! that sounds terrible! how does that make me look! "you got one daughter and you can't even!" you think i never met a gay before, huh? you think the gays were invented for you and only you? NO. i meet this lesbian the other day? wow, she is so great. she does so much stuff. she has a dog and a wife and a small business she runs with a friend from college.

LUCY. i thought you thought being queer sucks.

JOE. NO. i did not say that.

LUCY. um –

JOE. harder. i said life it is harder, you are a lesbian.

it is also harder you are left-handed.

these are just facts!

left-handed scissors, left-handed desks. it is a pain in the ass, being the OTHER scissors.

we must be honest with each other!

LUCY. you don't want that.

JOE. did i not just say that?

LUCY. you don't actually want that.

JOE. you are twenty-one. you are an adult. i will treat you as an adult! an equal.

(**LUCY** *decides to test this.*)

LUCY. okay then. pull over there.

JOE. pull over where?

LUCY. there. take that turnoff.

JOE. that is not a good place to stop.

LUCY. take that turnoff.

(**JOE** *tries to brush her off. an "okay, you got me!" energy.*)

JOE. that is a good example! a very good example.

LUCY. i'm serious.

JOE. you want to stop? i will stop.

(*he keeps driving.*)

LUCY. okay.

(*he keeps driving.*)

JOE. i will stop.

Scene 8

(split scene.)

*(***JENNY*** *is at a bar with a beer. maybe out in the bar's backyard patio!)*

*(***LUCY*** *drinks from her beer. she smokes. maybe in the same bar. it's a little loud in the bar. maybe live music is playing tonight!*)

JENNY. everything.

i had everything.

you can't even imagine how much i had.

my house? growing up?

but i wasn't a boy.

and there was a day.

it was early.

i was young.

there was a day when i looked around and thought, "oh."

"i see."

"i get it now."

"you will have all this, but it will never be yours."

"you stay here, it will never be yours."

LUCY. portland.

we're from portland.

---

* A license to produce *Young Americans* does not include a performance license for any third-party or copyrighted music. Licensees should create an original composition or use music in the public domain. For further information, please see the Music and Third-Party Materials Use Note on page iii.

well, neither of us are from portland, actually.

my dad and i used to joke, what a shame it was that neither of us could run for president.

but –

we run a bird shop.

bird shop.

it's like a, store? for birds?

it's also kind of a hospital?

JENNY. we met at a wedding.

sorry, that was your original question.

we met at a wedding.

a cousin i'd never been close to growing up.

i'd just graduated, there were no jobs.

not that there had been before.

LUCY. no, he was a professor.

and one day, he just decided to, just out of the blue –

actually no, it was –

it was right after my mom left us?

that he decided to – do something else with his life, i guess.

JENNY. so this guy, this new guy?

an émigré with a green card?

why not?

LUCY. every day he had gone to work in a suit and tie

– i didn't even think he owned sneakers –

but then one day i saw him coming out of the shop in an apron and a name tag and i was like, "oh."

LUCY. "this."

"this is what you were meant to do."

Scene 9

> (**JOE** *catches* **LUCY** *smoking. maybe around the corner at a gas station.*)

JOE. so you smoke now?

> (**LUCY** *whirls around, caught.*)

LUCY. what?

JOE. oh ho ho. you think you can hide yourself from me!

LUCY. no.

JOE. smoker.

LUCY. not really, no. no. sometimes?

JOE. you gonna smoke this nice gas station up! this place used to be a shithole, now it is nice and now they are not going to invite us back!

LUCY. fine –

JOE. hit me.

LUCY. what?

JOE. you got one for your dad?

LUCY. i thought this place was nice.

JOE. you have already blown it.

LUCY. you don't smoke.

JOE. you don't know! maybe back at the shop, maybe me and kevin? you don't know.

LUCY. you don't smoke.

JOE. a year goes by, who knows what i am up to!

LUCY. you have asthma.

JOE. so?

> *(**LUCY** hands him a cigarette. **JOE** smokes, too. he doesn't really like it. awkward. he doesn't know how to hold it.)*

LUCY. you're not holding it right.

JOE. that is how i hold it!

LUCY. here.

> *(she helps him.)*

JOE. where did you learn this?

LUCY. it wasn't hard.

everyone smokes out there.

or at least more people smoke out there than here, i guess.

it was the easiest way to practice my language skills. people don't mind you standing there if you're also smoking.

it was like my test.

like, can i bum a cigarette without them knowing?

can i just blend in?

i mean, the answer was no. never. but –

maybe?

for a moment, it was like, "yeah. maybe i belong here."

> *(beat. **JOE** absorbs this.)*

JOE. so maybe later, we do some drugs.

LUCY. whaaaat? i'm not doing that.

JOE. no! it is legal now! *(beat.)* i think?

LUCY. no, like i'm not doing that with you.

JOE. you think you are the only cool one?

long time ago, i used to, all the time!

first time, this guy come over to the house, from the university, he say, "wow, welcome to oregon, nice to meet you! you want to smoke? we smoke!"

– i am new on faculty, i want to be friendly, so i say, "okay, we smoke."

i think it is cigarettes.

wow, it is not cigarettes.

i do all sorts of things before you were born, you would not even know!

LUCY. riiiight.

JOE. see? old dogs, new tricks!

LUCY. we are never doing this again.

JOE. you got it.

LUCY. this did not happen.

JOE. copy that, chief.

(they smoke together.)

Scene 10

*(next morning. at a gas station. **JENNY** gets back into the car. she looks slightly hungover and crabby.)*

JENNY. that place was disgusting.

(she hands him a dollar.)

JOE. you didn't make a purchase?

JENNY. didn't have to!

JOE. but i told you –

JENNY. didn't ask me! didn't even turn his head.

JOE. you should have bought something.

JENNY. i saved you a dollar, professor!

*(**JOE** starts the car, pulls out of the gas station.)*

there was no toilet paper. someone had vomited in the corner. clearly not worth a dollar.

JOE. please don't do that next time.

JENNY. why?

JOE. HERE in this COUNTRY, it's generally accepted that you should make a purchase before using the facilities. it's an unwritten contract.

JENNY. who said that?

JOE. it's just the custom.

JENNY. that's a ridiculous custom.

JOE. you use the bathroom, you buy something. you go to a restaurant, you tip.

JENNY. i what?

JOE. you leave extra money for the server. a service charge.

JENNY. how much?

JOE. fifteen percent. sometimes more. probably more.

JENNY. i have to pay for my food and then i have to pay MORE for my food?

JOE. for your server. it's how they make money.

JENNY. they don't get paid by the owner?

JOE. not really, no. so you have to make sure they get paid.

JENNY. that's bullshit. i'm not doing that.

JOE. well, you should!

JENNY. so i don't tip, what happens, they come after me?

JOE. it's just polite. it's just – you know? forget it. forget it!

JENNY. you are so afraid.

JOE. ha HA!

JENNY. you are so afraid of what everyone is going to think!

JOE. yes! of course! why wouldn't i be? the only way you get anything in life is people and what they think! i go to a faculty meeting, i go to a review. whether i get promoted, whether i get more money, another job, a BETTER job, a job that allows me to do more of what i want and less of what i hate? that is one hundred percent people and what they think. especially when you're still an adjunct –

JENNY. you keep saying, what is that?

JOE. it means i'm temporary. it means any time they want to get rid of me? without tenure, goodbye!

JENNY. then get tenure.

JOE. it doesn't work like that.

JENNY. it has to do with "people and what they think."

JOE. yes!

JENNY. so when people ask you, when people ask you about us, what will you say?

JOE. what?

JENNY. "people and what they think."

JOE. we met at a wedding.

JENNY. but that wasn't – i mean, we both KNEW –

JOE. knew what?

JENNY. we were arranged.

JOE. oh. OW. is that what you think this is?

JENNY. come on, my auntie knew your auntie –

JOE. but that's not the same thing as "arranged."

(**JENNY** *gives him a look.*)

JENNY. i mean, if you'd been disgusting, i wouldn't have come.

JOE. thanks.

JENNY. they showed me a picture, beforehand. i didn't go in BLIND, i'm not stupid.

(*beat.*)

JOE. not stupid, huh?

JENNY. what?

JOE. where were you last night?

JENNY. what?

JOE. i woke up and your bed was empty.

JENNY. i couldn't sleep. i got bored. i went across the street to the bar.

JOE. you went to a bar?! that is so dangerous!

JENNY. no, the guy serving drinks, he's half. his mom's from where i'm from. so i could actually TALK to someone instead of just –

JOE. he was just trying to sell you a drink.

JENNY. he gave it to me for free!

JOE. oh, so you were in there begging for drinks –

JENNY. i didn't have to beg.

JOE. did you even tip?!

JENNY. you're an adjunct, you have no money! *(beat)* you want me to go back? hand him a dollar? come on, you were right around the corner.

JOE. but i wasn't THERE. i woke up and i had no idea where you were, no idea who to ask.

JENNY. who do i know in – where are we now? – tennessee? arkansas?

JOE. i don't know who you know, i don't know what you'd do or how to get you back if something happened to you. *(beat)* so PLEASE DON'T DO THAT.

    (silence settles over them. the tape stops.)

can you flip the tape?

JENNY. sure. listen to more of your FAVORITE songs.

JOE. ha HA.

JENNY. what?

JOE. these aren't my favorite songs.

JENNY. we keep playing them.

JOE. these songs are for you. to learn english.

JENNY. riiiight.

JOE. you think i like these songs?! these songs are GARBAGE!

JENNY. mm hm.

JOE. i have JBL speakers. i don't care about music and i have JBL speakers in back?

JENNY. what does that prove?

JOE. okay, i'm going to pull over.

JENNY. what?! you can't pull over here!

(he changes lanes suddenly.)

okay, okay! i believe you. i believe that you don't like shit music –

JOE. look in back.

JENNY. where?

JOE. in the back.

JENNY. what am i looking for?

JOE. it's a shoebox. it's black.

(she pulls something from out of the trunk.)

JENNY. okay.

JOE. the one written in green, there's a tree in the corner.

JENNY. this one?

JOE. play it.

JENNY. why?

JOE. you think i'm just top 40? you think this is my music? okay. so play it.

(she ejects the first tape, puts in this different tape. music. even before we can figure out what song this is –)*

fast-forward.

JENNY. what?

JOE. that song's not very good.

JENNY. i thought you were showing me YOUR music.

JOE. just fast-forward to the next one.

(she does.)

fast-forward.

fast-forward.

fast-forward.

fast-forward.

no, wait, rewind, go back.

JENNY. to where?

JOE. beginning of the song. rewind. rewind. stop.

(she does. they listen. we can't place the song at first. and yet, he waits, expectantly.)

JENNY. …i know this.

JOE. what?

JENNY. this song, i know this.

---

* A license to produce *Young Americans* does not include a performance license for any music by Davie Bowie. The publisher and author suggest that the licensee contact ASCAP or BMI to ascertain the music publisher and contact such music publisher to license or acquire permission for performance of the song. If a license or permission is unattainable for music by Davie Bowie, the licensee may not use the song in *Young Americans* but should create an original composition in a similar style or use a similar song in the public domain. For further information, please see the Music and Third-Party Materials Use Note on page iii.

JOE. *(beat)* no, you don't.

JENNY. i do. i have this album at home.

JOE. david bowie?

> *(this may be a davie bowie song or something like it.)*

JENNY. ...yes?

JOE. NO, YOU DON'T.

JENNY. what?!

JOE. SHUT YOUR MOUTH, NO, YOU DON'T!

> *(that was a little aggressive.)*

JENNY. what, i can't know him?!

JOE. no, no, no! it's just – you know this song?

JENNY. yes.

JOE. you have the album.

JENNY. not on me, no.

JOE. nobody knows this song. this song is like, twenty years old.

JENNY. well, i know it.

JOE. you like it?

JENNY. yeah.

JOE. what do you like about it? him.

JENNY. other than the fact that he is a hot man?

JOE. he so is.

JENNY. he's

he's an alien.

he's a space explorer.

he comes from somewhere else and chooses to make this his home.

and yet, he gets to be exactly who he wants to be.

and that's me.

JOE. *(suddenly)* would you like to go on a date?

JENNY. what?

JOE. *(knee-jerk reflex)* what?!

i mean, would you like to go out on a date. with me?

JENNY. okay.

JOE. okay?

JENNY. you didn't hear me the first time?

JOE. i just wanted to double check.

JENNY. okay.

JOE. okay! i will see you later then. on our date.

(he keeps driving.)

Scene 11

*(**JOE** waits. **LUCY** comes back to the car.)*

JOE. well?

LUCY. closed.

JOE. what?!

LUCY. till july. construction.

JOE. how can that be?

LUCY. well, did you check the website?

JOE. no. why would i do that?

LUCY. so you want to move on?

*(but **JOE** is still emotionally wounded.)*

JOE. closed. how can it be closed?

LUCY. come on, it's not even worth seeing.

JOE. have you seen it?

LUCY. it's a line and another line drawn by some guys in a room somewhere else that they drew just because.

JOE. yes. and now we're here to see it.

LUCY. it's overrated, i'm sure.

JOE. it is the place of possibility! colorado, utah, arizona, new mexico. and for a single moment until you have to move for the next person's turn, YOU, you get to exist in all four places at once! i want us to remember we were here.

LUCY. we will.

JOE. not if we are not actually on it.

LUCY. well, according to google maps, we're at the four corners monument. we're roughly in the vicinity. so i think that counts.

JOE. we are in the parking lot. we cannot get a photo op from the parking lot.

LUCY. why not?

JOE. there is a medallion on the ground that tells you where the spot is. that is how you know that you are there.

LUCY. says who?

JOE. it is the rules.

> *(beat.)*

LUCY. stand there.

JOE. what?

LUCY. that crack. stand over it.

JOE. lucy –

LUCY. just do it.

> (**JOE** *does.* **LUCY** *takes a picture of him with her phone.)*

there. four corners. we did it.

JOE. *(beat)* but that is not actually THE four corners.

LUCY. so?

JOE. well, when we tell people, we went to four corners?

LUCY. we did. right there.

JOE. but it's not THE four corners.

LUCY. it's the four corners i went to. with my dad.

Scene 12

(outside an IHOP. **JENNY** *bursts out of the
IHOP.* **JOE** *follows.)*

JENNY. what the fuck!

JOE. well, i wasn't hungry anyway.

JENNY. what the fuck is wrong with you?!

JOE. me?! i didn't do anything.

JENNY. yeah! you just stood there.

JOE. sat. i sat there. we were eating pancakes, so i wasn't
really standing, per se –

JENNY. how could you let that happen?

JOE. come on, they were kids. don't worry about it.

JENNY. they were drunk.

JOE. exactly! they were drunk kids. let's go, let's get out of
here. let's finish our date somewhere else.

JENNY. i forgot my jacket.

JOE. don't go back in there.

JENNY. it's my fucking jacket SO i am going back in there.

JOE. I'LL go get it. i'll ask the waitress. she'll probably be
happy to see me, i left a good tip.

JENNY. wait, you gave that bitch a TIP?

JOE. of course. were you not listening before? they don't
make a living wage, so you have to.

JENNY. of course you paid for dinner. and tipped. of course.

JOE. yeah of course! you have to. you can't NOT pay for
your food.

JENNY. do you want to be an adjunct your whole life?

JOE. *(confused)* i don't know what that has to do with dinner, but that is not part of the plan, no.

JENNY. then you're going to go in there with me and you're going to TELL THEM that we want to finish eating the food we paid for.

JOE. we can't do that. please don't make me do that. they've probably cleared away all the food by now anyway!

JENNY. well then, i'll go in without you.

JOE. and do what? yell at them, fuck them up?

JENNY. YES.

JOE. NO.

JENNY. so you don't want to go back in there and get your ass handed to you by those dudes?

JOE. no, i do not want my ass handed to me by anyone. ever.

JENNY. you're a pussy.

JOE. what?

JENNY. some fucking nerd. whose hobby is BIRDS!

JOE. birds are a diverse and fascinating species!

JENNY. class.

JOE. what?

JENNY. "birds are a diverse and fascinating class." not species. CLASS.

JOE. wait, is that right?

JENNY. you think you're the only one who knows anything about anything?

JOE. omigod, you're right. you're absolutely right.

JENNY. keep the car warm for me.

JOE. i can't let you go in there by yourself.

JENNY. why not?

JOE. you're my wife.

JENNY. not yet. not ever, maybe!

JOE. stop saying that. stop threatening me.

JENNY. how am i –?!

JOE. that's all you've done since we got in this car.

JENNY. well, maybe if you'd ASKED me whether i wanted to get in that car in the first place! you don't know a single thing about me! my life, my family, whether i even want kids.

JOE. *(beat)* you want kids, right?

(**JENNY** *throws her hands up.*)

you can't NOT want kids.

JENNY. you want kids so much? have them without me!

JOE. you think i would bring you out here, go to all this trouble, if i could have a family without you?

JENNY. you don't need someone else to have a kid.

JOE. um, yes. yes, you do. maybe YOU don't need someone else, but me? yes. i definitely do.

JENNY. you realize you would hate having kids.

JOE. um. no.

JENNY. yes! you would! you'd never be able to control them, your head would explode.

JOE. don't put words in my mouth.

JENNY. but then again, i'm the one letting myself be toted around the country by some nerd i just met, whom i'm not even one hundred percent sure about, so hey!

JOE. then WHY did you come here to marry me if you weren't even sure?!

JENNY. i thought you were cute!

JOE. what?

JENNY. i thought you were fucking cute, okay?! i thought you were like, a fucking cute-looking person.

with that cute fucking garden.

JOE. you've seen the garden?

JENNY. the picture they showed me of you was in the garden.

surrounded by squash and zucchini and beans and herbs and –

it looked like you were someone who cared for things. who could make things grow.

JOE. *(shrugs)* it's not that hard. oregon. things grow.

JENNY. i can't do that. i only make things wither and die.

but you?

so i saw it, and i thought, "okay! why not! why not meet the man with the squash and the kind face and see what happens. why not go see his garden?"

what would it be like to be with someone like that?

> *(beat.)*

JOE. okay.

JENNY. what?

JOE. let's go.

> *(he takes off his jacket.)*

JENNY. what're you doing?

JOE. i'm getting ready to back you up. but i like this jacket very much. so i'm gonna take it off first.

(he rolls up his shirt sleeves.)

JENNY. have you ever been in a fight before?

JOE. no. but here i go.

(he balls up his fist.)

JENNY. you're gonna hurt yourself.

JOE. i am well aware.

JENNY. you hit someone with your fist like that, and you're gonna break your hand.

JOE. how?

JENNY. your thumb. you can't put your thumb under your fingers.

JOE. how do you know that?

JENNY. i've got four brothers.

JOE. oh wait, and the shirt. i should take off the shirt, too.

(he takes off his button-down shirt.)

it's my one good shirt, the rest are at home. and the shoes!

JENNY. seriously?

JOE. these are my best shoes.

(he takes off his shoes.)

how do i look?

JENNY. ridiculous.

JOE. we're going to fight some sixteen-year-olds in an IHOPE. we're already ridiculous.

Scene 13

*(**JOE** scans a strip mall.)*

JOE. how HOW is this possible? the IHOPE it was right here. it was right here.

LUCY. twenty years is a long time. businesses close.

JOE. no. but also yes. and to be replaced by a starbucks!

LUCY. i thought the cake pops were really similar. for what it's worth.

JOE. but it was the IHOPE! the one where your mother she decided i was not so bad.

LUCY. wait, THAT was your first date. you could've taken her anywhere and you took her to IHOP?

JOE. the prices they were quite reasonable! i wanted to take her somewhere where she could have anything she wanted. and then! *(fondly)* they ban us for life.

LUCY. so in a way, you outlasted them.

JOE. i did! i did, huh?

(to where IHOP used to be) try to ban me now, bitches!

(a nice moment.)

LUCY. so you want to hear something weird?

...

i think i want to go back.

*(**JOE** looks behind him.)*

JOE. where?

LUCY. back.

*(**LUCY** gives him a look. **JOE** gets it.)*

JOE. you were out there for a whole year. you just came back.

LUCY. i know.

JOE. you did the walkabout. you got your cigarettes. you got to hang out. what else is there?

LUCY. i think i – i want to look for my birth parents.

JOE. and how would you do that?

LUCY. before i left, i emailed my advisor. i asked her about what it would look like. taking a semester off.

JOE. a semester?

LUCY. or a year.

JOE. but you still have senior year. you're supposed to be graduating in a year.

LUCY. i know.

JOE. so you think, "oh, i will go. oh, i will come back."

and everything will just wait for you?

LUCY. it's called a gap year.

JOE. it's called maybe you don't graduate.

LUCY. people do that.

people take gap years.

JOE. WHITE PEOPLE do that! white people take gap years. not you.

LUCY. if i don't go now, i'll never do it.

JOE. what will you do? where will you look?

bum a cigarette and say, "yo man, you seen anyone who looks like me?"

LUCY. ...

JOE. tell me how.

tell me how you are going to do this.

LUCY. i don't know. i haven't really thought this through.

JOE. apparently not!

LUCY. you don't know what it's like.

JOE. i don't know what it's like?

to be kicked out of a place that does not want you?

that does not need you?

LUCY. i know this is hard to believe, but this is not about you.

JOE. i am your family. you want a new family.

okay!

this is not about me? then who is it about?

LUCY. i hate how you do this.

you play dumb and then you make me feel like shit for wanting what i want.

JOE. when have i done this?

LUCY. no one else does this to their kids, you know?

nobody!

every little piece of my life, i have to consider you.

sometimes i think you just got me because you couldn't bear to be lonely!

so you could have someone who couldn't leave you.

JOE. if i cannot give you quality time, at least i will give you quantity time.

LUCY. omigod, this is why you need your own friends! i can't be your friend all the time!

JOE. how you know i don't got any friends?

LUCY. well, do you? where are they? no one i've seen.

>(*she realizes how mean this is, but sits in it anyway.*)

i can't be your whole world. it's fucking exhausting.

JOE. fine. go. if i could manage without your mom, i can manage without you.

LUCY. why do you think mom left in the first place?

JOE. you think i pushed your mom away?

LUCY. well, you certainly didn't make her want to stay.

>(**LUCY** *has gone too far. she knows it. she stops herself.*)

and this is why we can't be honest.

JOE. i guess not.

Scene 14

(**JOE** *and* **JENNY** *cram back into the car.*
JENNY *in the driver seat.*)

JENNY. shit shit shit shit!

JOE. omigod omigod omigod!

(*she starts driving.*)

what did we do? what did we just do?! omigod, i've never done anything like that before, wow, i hope no one's writing down our license plate! no one's gonna believe this. my colleagues're gonna freak out when i tell them all this.

JENNY. you threw a cup of water in his face!

JOE. no, i mean, like all of this. i didn't tell them about you. i just said i'm going on a road trip.

JENNY. why not?

JOE. i didn't want to jinx it.

JENNY. jinx it?

JOE. i thought you might change your mind. you still might! it just seemed like such a long shot that any of this would happen! you seemed – too good for me!

JENNY. hah.

JOE. and WHY. that's what i thought. "WHY would someone want to marry you? what about you does she not know? what have they not told her?"

JENNY. why're you always paranoid?

JOE. because! because your parents' love story is your own.

JENNY. oh, ew.

JOE. that's the only way you learn how to love someone. and my parents? not great.

JENNY. then how are there other kinds of love, if the only love story you know is the one your parents lived through?

JOE. *(realizes)* wait a minute!

JENNY. what?

JOE. you're driving this car.

JENNY. yes?

JOE. how did you do that?

JENNY. i put the keys in and i drove.

JOE. you can't drive this car. nobody knows how to drive this car. I'M the only one who knows how to drive this car.

JENNY. apparently not!

JOE. and you can't drive!

JENNY. i'm driving right now.

JOE. i mean, you're not licensed in america!

JENNY. we'll switch at the next exit.

JOE. THAT was the next exit. PULL OVER.

JENNY. you're going to get more attention drawn to us if you make me pull over right here.

JOE. slow down. SLOW DOWN.

JENNY. relax.

(**JENNY** *takes out weed, tosses it at him.*)

JOE. what is that?

JENNY. what does it look like?

JOE. where'd you get that?

JENNY. they owed us dinner. those fucking potheads owed us dinner, so –

JOE. we have to bring that back.

JENNY. why?

JOE. because! it's illegal to do that!

JENNY. it's illegal to fight in a restaurant?

JOE. yes?

JENNY. and it's illegal to steal drugs?

JOE. yes?

JENNY. and it's illegal to have them?

JOE. ...yes?

JENNY. so why would we go back?

JOE. that is, i guess, correct.

Scene 15

(**JOE** *sits outside, on a rock, birding. He's
got binoculars, but he's not looking through
them.* **LUCY** *finds him, sits next to him.
neither wants to talk first. finally –)*

LUCY. you missed one.

JOE. no, i didn't.

LUCY. right over there.

JOE. i see him.

LUCY. the robin?

JOE. it's not a robin.

LUCY. then what is it?

JOE. it is a lame-o. it is a lame-o bird, that's what it is. he
is hopeless.

LUCY. wonder what he's saying.

JOE. i know what he is saying. he is saying: "hey! hey!
i am needing a girlfriend! where is my girlfriend?
please hurry! imma die soon!"

LUCY. dad, are you high?

JOE. yes. i told you: later we do some drugs. i need the
chill out.

LUCY. well, that's true.

JOE. look at him out there very sad. boo hoo.

LUCY. little late for mating season.

JOE. well, he is a late bloomer. he is just trying to catch up,
okay? that is why he is so loud. desperate man!

(**LUCY** *squints at the bird.)*

LUCY. he's got a broken wing. he can't migrate. maybe that's why he's so desperate sounding.

JOE. no. he is desperate because he is looking for a date!

LUCY. why don't you date?

JOE. how you know i don't?

LUCY. so ARE YOU dating anyone?

JOE. ha HA.

LUCY. are you?

JOE. WHO would i date? where imma find them?

LUCY. you're a small business owner.

JOE. yeah! SMALL business. walmart, i am not.

LUCY. you're single, you're solvent, you're not that bad-looking.

JOE. but you did not say "good-looking!"

LUCY. you're your own boss. you're fucking crafty. you made all my halloween costumes. you GARDEN.

JOE. iiiiii don't know.

LUCY. you can date whoever you want, i don't care.

JOE. you don't care?

LUCY. okay, that was YEARS ago. i was how old?

JOE. ten! you are ten. i bring home a friend and you scream bloody murder.

LUCY. i thought they were strangers! "stranger danger." i know the difference now. you're a catch. *(shrugs)* you're technically a catch.

JOE. catch and release, that's what i am!

LUCY. you're not horrible to be around.

(they see some movement around the lame-o bird's nest.)

LUCY. ohp! look. what's that?

(a tiny bird pokes out of the nest.)

it's a tiny baby bird. i guess that's why he's not migrating. *(thinks)* he? she?

JOE. he.

LUCY. you ever see that before?

JOE. he is a northern flicker. that is what he does.

LUCY. oh.

(beat)

JOE. you think i can date? i cannot date. i am still married.

LUCY. you and mom are barely married.

JOE. that is still married!

LUCY. get a divorce.

JOE. why would i do that? i marry someone, i marry them for all time.

LUCY. it's just a piece of paper.

JOE. maybe i like my piece of paper.

*(**JOE** is silent.)*

you look just like her.

LUCY. who?

JOE. i am serious. you know that?

LUCY. okay. i mean, i don't see how that's true. since that is biologically impossible. but okay.

JOE. i wish it were not so.

(beat)

i am thinking of closing the shop.

LUCY. what?

JOE. find a buyer. sell it, maybe.

LUCY. you can't do that.

JOE. why not?

LUCY. don't sell the shop.

JOE. maybe i take a gap year. why not?

LUCY. you love that store.

JOE. and maybe i, too, can let it go.

(he lets this weigh on her. he exits.)

Scene 16

(**JOE** and **JENNY** *smoke up the stolen weed
under the stars.*)

JENNY. if this is camping, camping is ridiculous.

JOE. what're you talking about?! camping is amazing!

JENNY. who invented camping, i want to know. who
decided their house wasn't enough, that they needed to
leave their house and go out and sleep among the trees.

JOE. under the big open sky!

(**JENNY** *takes out weed, rolls a joint.*)

how do you know how to do that?

JENNY. you think we don't have this back at home?

JOE. we grew up two hours from each other. how do you
know so much more of the world than me?

JENNY. you got to do whatever you wanted growing up.
i didn't. so i sought them out.

(*she lights the joint.*)

JOE. give it to me.

JENNY. you don't have to impress me.

JOE. believe me, i am not going to impress you.

(*she hands him the joint.*)

what do i do?

JENNY. you inhale. like a cigarette.

JOE. (*nods, then*) i also don't smoke cigarettes.

JENNY. you just breathe.

JOE. just breathe.

JENNY. just breathe.

(he inhales. beat, waits.)

JOE. i don't feel anything.

JENNY. give it some time.

JOE. no, like i don't FEEL my – is my face numb?

JENNY. you just started. wait.

JOE. okay.

(he waits. as they do –)

JENNY. marry fuck kill.

JOE. what?!

JENNY. that's a game.

JOE. i've never heard of this game.

JENNY. it's an american game, some american came up with it.

JOE. if it was american, i think i would've heard of it.

JENNY. my brother taught me. so. marry fuck kill.

JOE. i don't think i'm going to like this game!

JENNY. shouldn't we know each other if they're going to ask us questions?

JOE. immigration is not going to ask us that.

JENNY. you don't know. so: marry fuck kill.

JOE. those are all bad!

JENNY. marry is bad?

JOE. i'm already married!

JENNY. we're not married yet.

JOE. i am SOON TO BE MARRIED.

JENNY. so the game, i say any name, living or dead, and you say if you'd rather marry, fuck, or kill the person.

JOE. aaaaaah, i don't want to say that!

JENNY. you want to learn things about each other? let's go. *(starts)* meryl streep.

JOE. i can't marry meryl streep.

JENNY. it's a GAME.

JOE. she wouldn't want to marry me! she'd have so many other options.

JENNY. she doesn't get a say in it.

JOE. oh, i don't like that either.

JENNY. you have to choose!

JOE. ...marry. then quickly divorce. she has so many more important things to do.

JENNY. indira gandhi.

JOE. NO.

JENNY. i didn't say GANDHI gandhi. i said indira gandhi.

JOE. what about you?

JENNY. me?

JOE. indira gandhi. marry fuck kill.

JENNY. fuck. obviously.

JOE. oh, obviously.

JENNY. so obviously fuck.

JOE. really?

JENNY. india's first female prime minister? she's a boss.

JOE. *(aside)* she's also dead.

JENNY. living or dead, that was the prompt! your turn.

JOE. stevie nicks.

JENNY. who's he?

JOE. OH.

JENNY. what?

JOE. you know meryl streep, you know david bowie, but you don't know stevie nicks?! fleetwood mac?!

JENNY. he was not on tv growing up, no.

JOE. SHE. she went out with lindsay buckingham. she being stevie. he being lindsay. very confusing, i know, but – marry fuck kill.

JENNY. you gotta give me some context here. what's she like?

(he smiles.)

OHHHHH.

JOE. what?! what?!

JENNY. OHHHHH. i see what this is.

JOE. what?! no. this is just a game.

JENNY. okaaaaay.

JOE. i used to have her poster on my bedroom wall growing up.

JENNY. i'll BET you did.

JOE. *(shrugs)* she's very talented.

JENNY. so?

JOE. SO she wouldn't like me. in real life, it would be very awkward between the two of us.

JENNY. you're selling yourself short.

JOE. she's a blonde witch who would probably find me boring!

JENNY. you never know if you don't ask.

> *(beat)*

JOE. can i hold your hand?

JENNY. hah.

JOE. okay. sorry!

JENNY. no! no, it's – just so weird that you asked.

JOE. i don't know!

i am just trying to figure out what the ground rules are.

nobody tells me what to do.

before i left for home, my father, the only advice he gave?

"you find a wife? don't let her talk too much."

i don't want to be like that. but i also don't know what else to be.

JENNY. now kiss me.

JOE. what?!

JENNY. but you have to stop smiling.

JOE. why?!

JENNY. you can't kiss me if you're smiling.

JOE. can i kiss you?

JENNY. YES.

JOE. okay.

JENNY. JUST DO IT.

JOE. all right.

JENNY. now you're making ME nervous!

JOE. you?!

JENNY. yes.

JOE. they say, if you're nervous, it's only because you don't know how it's going to go. so what you need to do to not feel nervous? – is visualize the future. see what will happen ahead of time, prepare for every single eventuality, and then not only will you become a more prepared candidate, but it may relieve stress in the moment – is what i read somewhere. so i'm just imagining us in about five to ten minutes. is that helping?

JENNY. and what are you imagining?

> (**JOE** *visualizes five to ten minutes from now.*)

JOE. oh. um. i don't know if i want to say –

> (**JENNY** *kisses him.*)

Scene 17

(a bell jangle. joe's bird shop in portland. **JENNY,** *older now, stands there. taking it all in.)*

LUCY. *(offstage)* coming!

> *(***LUCY*** *carries buckets of bird feed. she drops them at the sight of* **JENNY.***)*

hi.

JENNY. hi.

> *(***JENNY*** *now speaks with an accent. they're speaking english, this is her second language.)*

i guess i should've called first.

LUCY. you don't have a phone.

JENNY. so this is the shop.

LUCY. this is your shop, you know.

he built it because of you.

JENNY. he always had this dream.

LUCY. but you. you left and – he realized he didn't need to impress you anymore. he could do something else.

JENNY. do the birds like it here?

LUCY. they'd better.

JENNY. they don't get bored? it seems rather small.

LUCY. there's a bigger section in back.

JENNY. do they ever get to leave?

LUCY. why would they leave?

JENNY. so they can't.

LUCY. they were born into it, most of them. most of them, we get early on because they've been found somewhere. abandoned, brought here. most of them don't know anything else. so they can't survive out in the wild.

JENNY. such a shame.

LUCY. i don't think so. i don't think it's a shame to have somewhere to be.

JENNY. they are wild creatures. they are born out in the wild, they should die there as well.

LUCY. so what are you doing here?

JENNY. i wanted to see you before you left.

LUCY. what?

JENNY. junior year. you're doing study abroad?

LUCY. how do you know that?

JENNY. i'm technically still listed on your school forms. so they send me updates.

LUCY. that's rich.

JENNY. when are you leaving?

LUCY. i'm not.

JENNY. you got in.

LUCY. i applied. doesn't mean i have to go.

JENNY. you applied. because you finally want to see where you are from.

LUCY. and i changed my mind.

JENNY. what will you do instead?

LUCY. portland. i can stay in portland. like a normal person.

JENNY. if you need to leave, he will understand.

LUCY. ha HA! then you don't know him at all.

do you remember what dad was like when you left?

no. of course you don't. you weren't there.

a year.

it took him a year to get over you.

a year for him to be okay.

JENNY. i know that was hard.

LUCY. you don't know the half of it. you left him.

JENNY. i set him free.

LUCY. how does that work?

JENNY. he never would have had all this otherwise.

(a bell jangles.)

LUCY. okay, he's gonna be back soon. you need to go.

*(**JENNY** looks at **LUCY**, hard.)*

JENNY. why not?

why not see who you are?

why not make that choice?

LUCY. not all of us get these choices.

JENNY. you should choose every day of your life. for yourself.

LUCY. in other words, think only of yourself.

JENNY. yes.

LUCY. ha HA, right.

JENNY. you know what the answer is.

*(**JENNY** disappears. **LUCY** is once again alone in the woods.)*

Scene 17

*(**JOE** and **JENNY** under the stars.)*

JOE. so what's wrong with you?

JENNY. you think there's something wrong with me?

JOE. well, there's definitely something wrong with me!

JENNY. like what?

JOE. everything! everything about me! i'm an adjunct. at a STATE SCHOOL. i live in PORTLAND. OREGON.

JENNY. i thought you liked it there.

JOE. sure, i like it. but who wants their daughter to be a professor's wife in a second tier city? *(beat)* except for your parents. that was nice.

JENNY. what, you liked them?

JOE. i liked that they liked me.

JENNY. they did not like you.

JOE. *(sad)* oh.

JENNY. i mean, why should they, they just met you? and why does it matter whether my parents liked you?

JOE. because! they're your family!

JENNY. did YOU like my family?

JOE. aaaah.

JENNY. you can say it. i love my brothers, but the rest of them? materialistic, status-obsessed hypocrites. my father wouldn't even let me move out of the house for college.

JOE. they wanted you around.

JENNY. my brothers, no problem, but as soon as i wanted to?

JOE. you're the girl! people're protective of girls.

JENNY. so when you showed up? oh yeah, they were happy to see you. you took a problem off their hands. nobody has to think of me out here. *(beat)* what about you?

JOE. i respect my family.

JENNY. that's different.

JOE. i appreciate them for raising me.

JENNY. ha, you hate them just as much as i hate mine.

JOE. that's not necessarily true.

JENNY. you're HERE, aren't you? the eldest son and you're out HERE.

JOE. they just, they don't need me. they have my brother.

JENNY. your YOUNGER brother.

JOE. yeah.

JENNY. how did that happen?

JOE. i don't know. they sent me here for college and then, when i came back, it was just...so obvious they didn't need me. but my brother? two years younger and he was already running the family business, getting married, having kids.

JENNY. your brother sounds cute. is he single?

JOE. no, he's taken.

JENNY. joke.

JOE. i went home and there was just no place for me. so i applied to grad school here, came back. maybe that was their plan all along. send me away, keep him around.

JENNY. if that was the plan, they're fools.

JOE. no, they're just practical. they knew what they wanted. and it wasn't me.

JENNY. well, they're missing out.

JOE. i think they all feel sorry for me, that i'm out here. alone.

JENNY. little do they know.

JOE. so here i am. portland! teaching! you! this is my life. and i don't even know if i was the one who chose it.

JENNY. so choose. make a choice. this isn't the life you chose? then choose something else.

JOE. i think it's a little late for me.

JENNY. it is never too late. every day of your life is a choice.

JOE. *(sudden)* you know you don't have to marry me.

JENNY. romantic.

JOE. no, i mean it. you don't.

JENNY. i'm already here.

JOE. it should be a choice. every day should be a choice. if you choose to – if you want to – i would want you to choose it.

> *(silence settles over them.)*

JENNY. i can't have kids.

BOOM.

there you go.

just so you know.

JOE. you don't want to?

JENNY. i can't. so. you get to decide.

JOE. decide what?

JENNY. if you still want to – ninety days, right? less than ninety? you want to know what's wrong with me? there it is.

(beat)

JOE. so. do you WANT kids?

JENNY. i just told you: i can't have them.

JOE. but that's – you realize that's a different question than what i'm asking, yes?

JENNY. ...yes.

JOE. so. do you want kids?

JENNY. *(thinks)* i – don't know.

Scene 18

(**JOE** *tries to un-jam the tape from his tape deck with, like, a butter knife or something.* **LUCY** *approaches him.*)

JOE. twenty years, twenty years i have had this car, no issues, no problems!

then you come home and STUCK.

you get it stuck.

LUCY. dad. shut up.

JOE. what?

LUCY. i need you to shut up.

JOE. you need me to shut up?

LUCY. don't say anything. you say anything and i'm not gonna be able to do this, so don't.

just don't.

just wait till i'm done.

(**LUCY** *faces* **JOE**.)

you cancel my flights.

you get in my business.

you show up at inconvenient times in inconvenient places and take me on the stupidest detours that interest you and only you.

you are paternalistic.

you are infuriating.

you are the kindest, most considerate person i've ever known.

i am who i am because of you.

and that will never change.

JOE. "as soon as you have them, your children they are learning to leave you.

and the one teaching them how to do it is you."

that is what your mother said.

LUCY. she would say that.

JOE. you want to go back.

LUCY. i have to.

i have to or i will regret this for the rest of my life.

JOE. you are not asking for my permission.

LUCY. no. i'm not.

JOE. and when will you be back?

LUCY. i don't know.

> *(the tape deck magically clears itself. music plays.*)*

JOE. oh hey!

LUCY. what happened?

JOE. what did you just do there?

> *(maybe it is david bowie's "young americans." maybe it's his "let's dance." many good options here.)*

> *(**JENNY** from the past appears.)*

---

* A license to produce *Young Americans* does not include a performance license for any music by Davie Bowie. The publisher and author suggest that the licensee contact ASCAP or BMI to ascertain the music publisher and contact such music publisher to license or acquire permission for performance of the song. If a license or permission is unattainable for music by Davie Bowie, the licensee may not use the song in *Young Americans* but should create an original composition in a similar style or use a similar song in the public domain. For further information, please see the Music and Third-Party Materials Use Note on page iii.

JENNY. dance.

> (**JOE** *is transported to a honky-tonk bar in idaho.*)

JOE. what?

JENNY. husband –

JOE. we're not married yet.

JENNY. husband, i order you to dance.

JOE. that's one more thing you should know about me. i don't dance. my parents –

JENNY. your parents are not you. you are fearless.

JOE. no, i'm not. i'm actually very afraid of everything. and we shouldn't be here.

JENNY. and yet, here we are. now come on. come on.

JOE. people are looking.

JENNY. let them look.

JOE. aaaaah. the song's almost over.

JENNY. but it's not done yet.

JOE. it's gonna end soon.

JENNY. it's always all going to end. so. why not? why not?

> (**JOE** *gives in. they dance.*)

End of Play

www.ingramcontent.com/pod-product-compliance
Lightning Source LLC
Chambersburg PA
CBHW070639120726

47909CB00004B/1503